KEVIN'S DICTIONARY

Life...

in a word

A picture is worth a 1,000 words...
but a word can be a whole new picture!

Life in a Word
Kevin E. West

For information, bulk orders, or to use this as a part of your training programs, please contact: TitleTown Publishing | P.O. Box 12093 | Green Bay, WI 54307-12093 920.737.8051 | www.titletownpublishing.com

Front cover design by Adam Donshik
Interior design and layout by Euan Monaghan
Design & Layout Editor | Travis J. Vanden Heuvel
Cover Photo by Ajay Jhaveri, Argentum Studios
Manuscript Photo by Claire Brueckner

Contact Publisher Tracy Ertl for all review, media, reprint inquires at (920) 737–8051 | tracy@titletownpublishing.com

Represented for Film and Television by Intellectual Property Group
Office of Joel Gotler | (310) 402–5154 | joel@ipglm.com
12400 Wilshire Blvd., Suite 500, Los Angeles, CA 90025

PUBLISHER'S CATALOGING-IN-PUBLICATION DATA
West, Kevin E.
LIFE IN A WORD / West.
– 1st edition. Green Bay, WI : TitleTown Pub., c2018.

ISBN: 978-0-9993574-5-3
10 9 8 7 6 5 4 3 2 1

DEDICATION

Dedicated to Dr. Marc Abrams, aka, "The Walking Man" of Silver Lake with whom I was walking when the idea of "Life in a Word" was born.

Thank you for all that you gave me – you are missed.

"I have found that if you love life, life will love you back."
— Arthur Rubinstein

THERE ONCE WAS A LITTLE BOY NAMED KEVIN...

Kevin naturally found himself observing life and having a word come to mind, but if he expressed his thoughts, other people gave him an odd look. Yes, he understood seeing a lovely picture and calling it "beautiful" or seeing two people laughing and labeling it "joy." But something was still missing for him. Kevin was seeking a larger appreciation of words and the spirit of their meaning in the context of life.

One day, he was laughing at his sister while she tried to swat a fly in the house. BAM! He found his answer in a common housefly, the only quick flying creature that sees human activity from both inside and outside...virtually everywhere. Suddenly, Kevin began to live his life and view it as if he were the 'fly on the wall.' Today, Kevin passes his perspective on to others in what he likes to call *Kevin's Dictionary.*

"A picture is worth a 1,000 words, but a word can be a whole new picture!"
- Kevin E. West

THE WORDS

Hope
Trust
Politics
School
Dance
Sport
Naked
Marriage
Lucky
Sex
Father
Wish
Noise
Trip
Playground
Work
Human

Home
Bath
Birth
Freedom
Intimate
Gift
Beauty
Respect
Wedding
Bed
Exercise
Love
Intelligence
Insurance
View
Island
Communication

Truth
Strength
Mother
Teacher
Precious
Peace
Religion
Time
Pressure
Passion
Perfect
Friend
Fight
Power
Extraordinary
Unique

Hope

\ hōp \

* to cherish a desire with anticipation

HOPE

Sometimes we seek world peace, or perhaps no morning traffic, but what about...

On a warm Saturday morning, an expensive sedan pulled up in front of a large, two-story colonial structure located in a quiet suburban part of town. The facility headmaster appeared and greeted the early 30s-ish smartly dressed couple. The couple was given a tour and provided a brochure with the typical daily curriculum. The couple seemed quite impressed with the amenities, the grounds and the lifestyle the facility clearly afforded its residents.

They moved to a meeting room where several file folders were spread across the table. Each folder contained photos, documents, medical history, background information, and on occasion a handmade piece of art. The couple sat down and set the facility brochure aside. From a distant makeshift corner hole in the wall, a young girl of maybe seven years peered through and squinted as the couple perused the folders.

The girl then pulled a mini-telescope from her pocket and continued to peep. The male visitor held up a file labeled *Jennifer,* and the girl smiled. He handed the folder to his wife and continued to peruse other folders. After a few minutes they picked up only two folders and handed them to the headmaster. Through her telescope, Jennifer could see that one of them was hers. She closed her eyes, smiled, and crossed her fingers.

Trust

\ trəst \

* assured reliance on the character, ability, strength, or truth of someone or something
* one in which confidence is placed

TRUST

Maybe you've shared a secret or looked for it in your lover's eyes, or...

A SMALL ENGINE CESSNA AIRPLANE shattered the serenity of a beautiful Sunday. Random small groups of participants stretched and engaged in light conversation. A 40s female scurried into a building for processing. She had several questions and the omnipresent release of liability to sign. The video that followed created more tension, which was now impossible to eradicate from her mind.

Outside, frenetic activity continued on the grounds, while a few hundred feet away in a back room, a pair of unknown hands quietly worked in confident rhythm. Strings, clips, metal and fabrics were intertwined in a maze of complex simplicity. The female participant suited up and met her instructor before the adventure took flight.

While she knew there was less than a one-in-a-million chance, the possibility remained: one is a really lonely number when it equals certain death. Nearby, deeply concerned loved ones looked on and hoped for the best possible outcome trying to understand the seemingly absurd necessity of this ritual. The instructor rejoined her, asked her to turn around, and in seconds, strapped on the parachute. Unlike going to a traditional airport, in this scenario, she was up and away in the plane in seconds. Only moments before, the chute contraption of safety was a pile of cloth and string in disarray, and its architect, an anonymous author of her eventual fate.

Politics

\ pä-lə-tiks \

* activities that relate to influencing the actions and policies of a government or getting and keeping power in a government
* the work or job of people (such as elected officials) who are part of a government

POLITICS

Elected folks who legislatively may control your fate, but then again...

AT 4:00 A.M., A MAN IN his early 50s was awakened from a dream. He sat up and realized it was a dream because he was still homeless in a stinky sleeping bag on the ground. Glass was suddenly shattered which sounded a nearby alarm. He jumped up and his sidewalk neighbor barked, "Don't get involved, ya fool!" He ducked behind a dumpster and watched. Moments later the predator breached the store with two filled pillowcases. A streetlight clearly revealed his face as the sound of sirens grew louder as they approached his location.

Initially when the police questioned Mr. Homeless he denied seeing anything. When morning dawned, the owner assessed the damage with the insurance adjustor. Once the adjustor was finished, Mr. Homeless entered the store, and the owner was very gruff, but softened when he learned the scruffy fellow could identify the robber. A conversation ensued and the two men shook hands as if equals.

It was near dusk on a winter's day at the police station when Mr. Homeless identified a mug shot, and the officer smiled. Soon the temperature would be way below freezing. At 4:00 a.m., Mr. Homeless awoke from a dream. But this time he rose from a small cot with fresh bedding and wasn't starving or cold. He stood up, exited the storage room of the previously pilfered store, and watched the snowfall from inside of his new home. Mr. Homeless smiled proudly.

School

\ skül \

* an organization that provides instruction;
an institution for the teaching of children

SCHOOL

Not every learning institution comes with homeroom and recess...

A couple of teenagers who'd been partying and drinking most of the night went cruising downtown. Around 2:00 a.m., the two teens barked out the window at a couple of hot ladies over 21, which caused the driver to swerve. Stealthily observing nearby was a motorcycle cop. He pulled the boys over and administered a breath alcohol test, which, of course, they both failed. Both boys were immediately arrested, including his fellow passenger for public drunkenness, and they were swept away to the county jail. The passenger's angry parents arrived quickly, posted bail, and took him home.

The young driver sat for well over an hour in the holding area waiting for his parents to arrive when his mother finally walked through the door. The boy was distraught and apologetic, well aware of his mistake. His mother cried, expressed her love, stood up and walked away as his father entered. The boy thought he was prepared for the worst. The father, however, gave his leg a light squeeze and said, "Don't worry son – you'll learn from this."

The boy said, "Yes, Dad, I promise I will." His father stood, started to step away from his son, then turned back and replied, "Yes, I'm quite certain you will. See you tomorrow." The father then gave his son a typical chuck on the arm, and walked out leaving the bewildered boy alone to spend the night...in jail.

Dance

\ dan(t)s, dän(t)s \

* to engage in or perform a dance
* to move or seem to move up and down
  or about in a quick or lively manner

DANCE

Maybe you're sitting in a theater about to watch your child perform, or imagine this stage...

THE DREAMY HOLIDAY ATMOSPHERE WAS suddenly cracked by the sounds of sirens. A family rushed from their home in a daze of smoke. Catching her breath, the mother realized one of her two children was not behind her. She screamed while her husband handed her the family dog and raced back inside to rescue their child.

Two fire engines arrived and 12 men leapt from the vehicles. Very few words passed between the firefighters but their bodies moved as if they were taking a Sunday stroll. Within seconds water gushed with rhythmic proficiency. The mother stood frozen in fear, tears streaming down her cheeks, clinging to her one child and their dog. Just then, in a blink and without words or a bullhorn, the seamless mythical silence of the scene changed.

The chorus line of firefighters shifted as glass shattered and a ladder was hoisted. A man suddenly jumped out of the window in virtual slow motion holding her child, and just behind him, she could see her husband stumble through, now wearing an oxygen mask. She moved from fear to joy as if a song had ended. Moments later, the fire was extinguished, the stage fell silent, the players slowed to their final positions, and the curtain of this great performance was drawn to a close with simplistic poetic grace.

Sport

\ sport \

* to amuse oneself; frolic to engage in a sport

SPORT

There is likely a score or at minimum some sweat and uniforms, or perhaps...

At 5:00 a.m., people from the United States woke up and prepared for game day. Adorned in various states of dress, based on their home location, they raced to their vehicles for the most anxiety-filled day of the calendar year. This game day was not one for sissies. You can't just randomly show up and see how it goes with so much on the line. The players must either be mentally strong and physically prepared or get squashed like a rotten tomato.

Many small children, having dreamt of this day, watched their grandmothers prepare from a distance. They've heard years of terrifying stories from their mothers but now it's time to shine or wilt. The clock struck 6:00 a.m. and a swarm of players descended upon various fields and locations. The thunderous forces were felt on the streets and reverberated throughout the formerly quiet neighborhoods.

Every strategy possible would have been mapped out once the bell sounded. Once the game starts, the challenge is if you could stay on your game in the face of such stiff competition. Once the doors fly open, the race of your life is on, because the veterans will have no mercy and you must emerge victorious. Within a few hours, the weak always fall by the wayside, but you have to remain strong. Welcome to Black Friday in America, people – the day after Thanksgiving and the biggest shopping day of the year. Bring your best and bring it on!

Naked

\ nā-kəd \

* not covered by clothing; nude; bare

NAKED

We all come into the world in our 'birthday suit'
so how can it be otherwise, well...

THE CONVENTION HALL WAS ALIVE with activity as the corporate team met on the mezzanine floor to complete their preparations. A junior male executive received a text message and excused himself. Fifteen minutes later, the elevator descended while the junior executive fumbled through a note pad looking like he'd just seen a ghost. He exited the elevator and a small gaggle of associates rushed toward him for an update. After a few words, his colleagues fell deathly silent. They noticed a pile of notes, which were not writ – ten by him, but moments ago handed to him.

The junior executive was about to enter the convention hall when an associate smacked him on the back, and said; "Jeez, thank God it's not me man. Ha, good luck." The convention room was packed with over a thousand suits that had been impatiently waiting for the keynote speaker. Backstage, clinching his trembling hands, he tried desperately to clear his dry throat.

Just as the speaker had managed to get his notes in order, his name was announced as the replacement speaker, causing him to drop the notes. As he stepped up to the podium, one of the pages he held slipped unnoticed by him to the floor. He couldn't see or feel anything, except for an odd draft that wafted between his legs. He could hear the applause, he could see the room, but he would have sworn that the audience was laughing at him.

MARRIAGE

\ mer-ij, ma-rij \

* an intimate or close union

MARRIAGE

One of life's most precious decisions en route to fulfillment, but then again...

THE LIGHTS DIMMED AND THE curtains parted in the stunning ballroom theatre, as the well-to-do crowd settled into their seats. The orchestra filled the room with a lovely perky melody, which prompted the choral dancers to move briskly onto the stage.

The dancers gracefully moved upstage and drifted from the foreground leaving two solitary figures. Like a feather riding on the wind, the couple effortlessly floated back and forth across the stage, entertaining their audience with every move. Their show was pure artistic dance poetry in motion. Their rhythm and flow was magical, and they both wore smiles most often associated with newly – weds the morning after the wedding.

For decades, the couple entertained their audiences with a grace and unity never before seen. As the years passed along, one could only marvel at their silhouette of oneness, connection and unified love – for their art and one another. Perhaps it was possible that a few of the couples in their audiences had equaled what these two accomplished on stage in an analogous, loving relationship, but it was doubtful. The incomparable union of Fred Astaire and Ginger Rogers, in so many ways, remains unsurpassed.

Lucky

\ lə-kē \

* having good luck
* happening by chance; fortuitous
* producing or resulting in good by chance; favorable

LUCKY

Maybe it was the name of your dog or how you felt in Las Vegas, or this...

THE YEAR WAS 1981, JUST a few months from high school graduation and freedom from their adolescent prison. Four energetic students were in the chemistry lab playing with some science toys. The smart-ass of the group quietly exclaimed, "Hey, I've got a great idea my uncle told me about." He grabbed a foot-long small rubber hose and placed it on the end of a gas tank port next to the sink. They then filled the sink with water and poured in some powdered soap.

They turned the knob and the water bubbled with gas. Quickly, the gas-filled bubbles rose well above the counter top. The smart-ass of the seniors said, "Ok, hand me a flint and everyone back up." The moment of truth had arrived when Mr. 'Idea Man' squeezed the flint. A spark hit the gaseous bubble mountain and caused a loud BOOM! The bubbles erupted into a massive eight-foot mushroom fireball cloud that instantly reached the ceiling.

For a moment, the flame took hold of the ceiling tile, and the students freaked the hell out because no one had considered that the ceiling tiles were made of flammable asbestos. The panic-stricken students clung to the table trying to avoid the reality of what would become of their futures should they burn the school down. After the longest ten seconds of their lives, however, the flame died out. The students exhaled with massive relief and disappeared into the hallway.

Sex

\ seks \

* either of the two major forms of individuals that occur in many species and that are distinguished respectively as female or male especially on the basis of their reproductive organs and structures
* the sum of the structural, functional, and behavioral characteristics of organisms that are involved in reproduction marked by the union of gametes and that distinguish males and females

SEX

The art of lovemaking, intertwined, sweating, panting – hungry for more, or...

EVENING ROSE AS THE SUN bid the day adieu and dipped behind the horizon. A couple in the twilight of life completed their evening walk and shuffled slowly up the long drive. They discussed memories that took them back to their early 30s when they had flown to Hawaii for their first glorious vacation.

The assisted living center entrance ramp greeted them, and they disappeared into the building. Back when she had fallen and broken her hip, they had decided it was no longer wise to live apart from others, nor from one another. She exited the bathroom in her nightgown. He glanced over with adoring eyes at the love of his life and ran his hand down the side of her beautiful cheeks. He found it terribly easy to remember exactly what it was like when her skin was as smooth as a newborn baby's back side.

As if 17 again, he slid his hands around her back like he was trying to undo her bra for the first time. His hands came to rest at her side and her hands once again joined his. He leaned down and gently nestled his nose into the corner of her neck, just below her ear, exhaling his warm breath onto her aging body. He softly kissed her skin. She virtually blushed and squeezed his hand, and they slowly stared into one another's eyes, the window of the soul, as the memories of their history rendered a deep soft kiss.

Father

\ fä-thər \

* a man who has begotten a child; sire
* God; the first person of the Trinity
* one related to another in a way suggesting that of father to child
* an old man —used as a respectful form of address

FATHER

The man who was your first rock, always there when you needed him, or...

TODAY, ON HER SPECIAL DAY, the stunning bride laughed with her wedding party during the final preparations, but her mother was oddly missing from the room. In a private library of the house, her mom sat alone holding a framed photo. She brushed her hand across the glass, which revealed a full family shot clearly from some years before – father, mother and daughter. Her tear fell.

Her father was a strong, proud, tremendous man and husband until his tragic unexpected death just five years before from cancer. While the mother had managed to carry on and find some semblance of happiness, on such a day as this a glaring gap existed. To retain tradition on her wedding day, both daughter and mother elected their favorite uncle to do the honors of giving her away.

Just then, the mother jumped to her feet, dialed her mobile phone, hung up and laughed out loud. She assisted her daughter for the next few hours, but then told a tall tale and disappeared. The 'down the aisle' moment approached and her mother was nowhere to be found. The organist began to play, and out of the corner of her eye, the bride spied her mother and gasped. The attendees turned to see the mother joining her daughter in her father's full dress military uniform. The mother's gait was as if she were military trained. She stopped, crisply turned at attention, draped her daughter's arm over hers and walked her down the aisle.

Wish

\ wish \

* to have a desire for (as something unattainable)
* to give expression to, as a wish; to give form to (a wish)
* to express a wish for; to request in the form of a wish; order
* to desire (a person or thing) to be as specified

WISH

Maybe you've rubbed a lamp for a genie
or even bought lottery tickets, or...

THE SCHOOL BELL RANG AND a slow moving fifth grade boy saw a mother talking with a teacher as her daughter, his classmate, stood nearby crying. The boy stayed close pretending to pick up a box of crayons he'd accidentally spilled.

When the mother and her daughter left, the little boy asked the teacher why his classmate was crying. The teacher explained to the boy that the little girl was very sick and had to go to the hospital for a long time. The boy asked if he could help, but the teacher explained that her illness specifically required the help of a blood related family member. He sadly understood and departed for home.

He stopped for a moment walking in a field, bent down, and pulled something from the field. Later in the day, the little boy told his mother about his classmate's situation and she took him for some ice cream to cheer him up. They entered the popular local ice cream joint and amazingly there sat the little girl. The boy grinned from ear to ear thinking that her parents wanted to cheer her up, too.

The little boy turned to his mom and said, "I'll be right back." He approached her table with his hands tucked behind him. The little girl smiled at his arrival. He extended his arm out to her, opened his hand, and placed a four-leaf clover next to her ice cream. He followed with, "I asked my mom if this would make me lucky enough to be your brother for a day because I'd like to give you that."

Noise

\ noiz \

* loud, confused, or senseless shouting or outcry
* any sound that is undesired or interferes with one's hearing of something
* an unwanted signal or a disturbance

NOISE

Simon and Garfunkel were far more right than we ever knew...

On an unusually warm Midwest morning, just after dawn, a couple scurried down to the kitchen. She had just hit 50 – he was closer to 60 – but they were both vibrant and active. Their three children had been born a year apart some 23 years ago. Two had already made their way out into the world. However, the poor economy meant that their youngest had only moved out yesterday.

The coffee was poured and some standard small talk ensued. They sauntered over to their favorite little breakfast bay window nook, which for decades had simply become a homework and study area, instead of its original purpose. They glanced out at the beautiful view, cherishing the sight of the finches that swooped in for a quick swig from the feeder mechanism.

They spoke of their long journey to commence and build a family. Naturally, the realization of never having lived without the hustle and bustle of kids clamoring about the house was mentioned. Without reason or cause, their talking ceased and they stared deeply at one another, mutually aware that a new chapter lay ahead. For the first time in more than 25 years, they both heard the echo of the fall wind softly bounce against the window, followed by an almost inaudible flutter of a bird's wing. They leaned back against the bay window frame and reveled in the joy of the deafening sound of silence.

Trip

\ trip \

* to dance, skip, caper, or walk with light quick steps
* to catch the foot against something so as to stumble
* to make a mistake or false step
* to stumble in articulation when speaking
* to make a journey

TRIP

Planes, trains and automobiles are not the only vehicles required sometimes...

A MIDDLE-AGED WOMAN, IN PREPARATION FOR the Spring Break visit from her college senior daughter, gardened in her backyard. The text message sound dinged on her phone and it read, "About two hours away – see you soon." She smiled at the anticipation of her daughter's visit and headed to the garage to stow her tools.

Sunlight beamed a spotlight onto a long since forgotten plastic bin labeled *Mom's old stuff* on the top of a tall storage rack. She smiled and reached for the bin when memories of the days of her own Spring Break from 30 years ago in Daytona Beach suddenly consumed her. In an instant, she could smell the ocean, hear the music and feel the sweat on her brow – throngs of college students' bodies, the boys, the beer, and the band.

She laughed alongside one of her sorority gal pals as they basked in the glow of being 22 carefree years old. The music in her mind raged when she wheeled around knocking over a stack of small clay potting shells onto the garage floor. The sharp sound of the shattered shards scattering snapped her back to the present day. She stood there amidst the wreckage on the floor, sort of laughed at herself, and noticed that just on the inside of the old box on the top was a cassette tape of the Rolling Stones – 'Can't Get No Satisfaction'.

Playground

\ play-graund \

* a piece of land used for and usually equipped with facilities for recreation especially by children
* an area known or suited for activity of a specified sort

PLAYGROUND

That favorite place of yours when you were a kid after school, or,...

HEREIN IS A WORLD THAT began over 200 years ago. Kings, queens, statesman, stars and other such luminaries have played in this sandbox. However, in this space on any given day, immense devastation is omnipresent. The harsh reality of this place has fostered its participants to develop destructive habits and pained appearances, even amidst hopeful anticipation. Still, this sandbox is highly revered and its toys are earpieces and phones. Everyday, for seven straight hours, a constant seesaw of emotion is illuminated by success or failure.

When the bell clangs, fast-paced decisions must be made. Information and instructions pierce the air, and the players in the sandbox point, reach for their notes and desperately try to get the attention of the other players. Suddenly, a moment of calm comes before the reeling numbers are reviewed and the pause gets tapped. Within a matter of seconds, the room goes from 0-100, in a blurred sense of reality, commerce and capitalism.

Approximately 533 people play in the sandbox at one time, but there are millions and millions of daily possibilities that can unfold. When the last bell of the day rings, the players must hand in their scorecards. With a respectful wink to one another, they say, "See ya' tomorrow." A stream of $1,000 suits exit the building and leave the New York Stock Exchange floor empty.

Work

\ wərk \

* activity in which one exerts strength or faculties to do or perform something
* sustained physical or mental effort to overcome obstacles and achieve an objective or result
* labor, task, or duty that is one's accustomed means of livelihood
* specific task, duty, function, or assignment often being a part or phase of some larger activity

WORK

A time clock, a career, a tough job
or a project for which we're paid, or...

SHE STUMBLED OUT OF BED and fell to the floor. No big deal; she was used to it. She turned on the bedroom lamp by the floor switch and scuffled over on her knees to scan her small, limited wardrobe to dress for a rare public meeting. She took 45 minutes just to remove her T-shirt and maneuver her body onto the shower chair because sitting in the bathtub hadn't ever been an option.

Over the next two hours, she labored in the kitchen to make breakfast, went back down her hallway to get dressed and prepared to walk outside. She exited the door, locked it with one hand and then struggled down the stairs without falling to go meet her pay-to-play driver. She arrived at her destination only to discover that it was a musty old building with no elevator or ramp to the second floor office. Seriously?

It took another 20 minutes for her to climb the stairs. She perspired through her clothes and had to stop many times to catch her breath. She held specially designed crutches that helped transport her oddly bent legs and small frame. Her day had begun at 6:00 a.m., and when she opened the office door, it was 1:00 p.m. Within 15 minutes, her meeting started and ended. She descended the stairs, a bit faster than going up, slid into the awaiting car utterly exhausted, and retraced the effort of returning to her couch.

Human

\ hyü-mən \

* of, relating to, or characteristic of humans; consisting of humans
* having human form or attributes
* susceptible to or representative of the sympathies and frailties of human nature

HUMAN

The mortal breathing beings that we all are,
but can we be more...

A FLOOD OF YOUTH AND immortality bolted from the school building at day's end in anticipation of tonight's high school football game. A nerdy merit scholar, who was constantly bullied, exited his classroom. Strangely he carried every book with him, as if at year's end, and began his daily solo walk home.

A popular pretty gal trailing in the hallway noticed he'd removed the lock and his locker was ajar. Curiosity led her to open the door and her face turned sour. She bolted out of the building, caught up with him and greeted him with a smile. The scholar nerd was fairly non-responsive but mumbled a few courteous replies. She offered some small talk and asked him if he were going to the football game.

"Of course not", he replied. "Well, what if we went together," she said. He lifted his head, "Really?" She agreed to pick him up at 6:30 p.m. that evening and they parted ways. At home he retrieved his high school annual and turned to the page that revealed the picture of the very same girl. He had written a note: "So pretty and popular, but yet, seems so nice." He sat quietly and smiled.

He removed a revolver from his backpack, went downstairs, and returned the gun to its proper place undetected by his parents. Simultaneously, the girl opened the note she found in his locker, held it to her chest, smiled and tore it up.

Home

\hōm\

* one's place of residence; domicile
* house
* familiar or usual setting

HOME

The safe haven that you depart from and arrive to everyday, or...

THE PLANE TOUCHED DOWN AFTER an extremely long business flight taking her half a world away from her family. While these trips were rare nowadays, with two kids headed to college, having two incomes was still necessary. The trips nonetheless took their toll on her physically and emotionally. Due to the time change, it was far too early to call back home to say, "Good morning." Twenty minutes later she reached her hotel, checked in, quickly drew a warm bath and settled into the prospects of the next few days of business with a glass of wine.

Despite exhaustion, she made the effort to unpack. She hung up her two business suits, and then cleared out the side exterior pockets of her main bag. She only removed the first few items of clothing and placed them in a dresser drawer. Just before closing the lid, she noticed an item in her bag she knew she hadn't packed. Upon closer examination, she lifted out her husband's oversized flannel shirt that she liked to sleep in during the colder winter season nights.

A wry smile filled her face as she pressed the flannel shirt to her cheek. She then buried her face in the shirt, took a deep breath, and inhaled the familiar scent. Instantly, she mentally traveled thousands of air flight miles and could feel herself wrapped in the arms of her entire family. She flopped onto the bed, clutched the garment tightly, closed her eyes and fell fast asleep.

Bath

\ bäth \

* a washing or soaking (as in water or steam) of all or part of the body

BATH

The soothing nature of crawling into the hot water and melting with it, or...

IN A SMALL CORNER OF a local park, the ugly neighborhood stray dog, Boney, appeared a bit bloated. Boney, aptly named for her severely under-nourished state, circled around and settled in a nice pocket of shade.

Boney's frail body began to shake and then convulse as if she were going to vomit. Kids playing nearby didn't notice because, "hey, it's just Boney." Five minutes passed and she struggled to her feet. She began to spin in a circle, whimpered lightly, and amazingly began to give birth. Boney cried loud enough to catch a little girl's attention as she tugged on her mommy's shirt and pointed. The mother urgently sent the daughter to retrieve a few bottles of water from the car. Upon her return, she witnessed the birth of Boney's last two puppies of seven.

They poured water over Boney and emptied the rest into a makeshift bowl. Boney was exhausted but leaned over for a few gulps. The little girl looked up at her mommy who called the Humane Society. Boney rose and instinctively began to paw at her pups and lick their eyes and mouths clean as they stretched out to grasp their first breath of life. The pups then nestled themselves, one by one, around the undernourished belly of their mother. As the mother and daughter stood nearby, Boney, depleted and under – nourished, gave each of her babies a few last licks of cleanliness.

Birth

\ bərth \

* the emergence of a new individual
  from the body of its parent

BIRTH

The sound of new life as the baby is handed to the exhausted Mother, or...

In the early morning hours of his 60th birthday, he stood alone before the pictures of his life – photos of his children, his family, and his friends alongside the images of his very successful career. A big day was planned with his folks, and many others who would be visiting town to celebrate this benchmark day. With his patriarchal expectations fulfilled, he found himself focused on what had eluded him. He grabbed his phone and called an old trusted friend, hung up, and smiled.

Later that night, the moment had arrived, "Speech...Speech," the crowd cried when he took the stage. He leaned into the microphone; his voice cracked and trembled, trying to fight the tears. He announced that earlier that day he had resigned from the CFO position he'd spent 30 years working to obtain. The crowd gasped in shock. The money, the security, and the prestige were now gone. Why?

He raised his hand, and the rumbling crowd fell silent. The birthday boy smiled when an unfamiliar man joined him on stage. The now ex-CFO stepped aside as this stranger took center stage to speak on his behalf.

"It gives me great pleasure to welcome the new assistant head football coach for Plainsview High School." The crowd erupted into cheers of joy knowing that 25 years ago, he'd walked away from his true love. He'd done himself proud, but now it was time for him to do what he was born to do.

Freedom

\ frē-dəm \

* the quality or state of being free
* the absence of necessity, coercion, or constraint in choice or action
* liberation from slavery or restraint or from the power of another

FREEDOM

The joy of your first night out after a long and difficult divorce, or...

A WOMAN ON THE BRINK of 40 sat anxiously in a waiting room. A male patient nearby noticed that she was quite buxom, and without realizing it, smiled at her chest before he raised his head to meet her unappreciative eyes. She extended a wry scowl towards him and her mind drifted back to her teen years and how popular she became when her chest developed before the other girls.

Like most, she initially enjoyed all the attention but grew to hate it over her lifetime. She'd certainly used her ample anatomy as an ally but also could recall so many fun things her endowment prevented along with being called sleazy. When her name was called, she rose with a slight sense of sad relief and greeted the doctor with a smile.

A few weeks later, for the first time since turning 17, she could actually see her shoestrings. She plopped into a chair and tied her shoes without having to prop her feet up on something. She stood in front of her bedroom mirror and admired the drastically reduced version of herself that stared back.

She tossed a bag filled with old bras on the sofa with a note that read, 'For Mary' and began to stretch. A few minutes later, she sent a quick text message that read, "See you in 30 minutes for coffee." She then put her phone away and enthusiastically took off to go for a jog...for the first time in her life.

Intimate

\ in-tə-māt \

* to communicate delicately and indirectly

INTIMATE

Two young lovers frolicking in the ocean before heading to the room, or...

A HEALTHY MAN IN THE prime of life emerged from the kitchen with chocolate milk and pie in hand. He joined his wife on the couch and placed the pie on her very large belly, clearly only weeks from childbirth. She plucked a little crust of pie from the plated piece he'd cut.

She noticed that he seemed uncomfortable so she set her milk down and took his hands. His throat was dry and his voice trembled when he began to speak softly. He confessed to his wife that the story he'd long since told her about his father was untrue. She remained still and concealed her internal concern at seeing him wracked in this level of discomfort. The truth was he'd never had a father, never knew him or met him, and she was stunned.

He was successful, attractive, and oozed with self-confidence. He moved his head back and forth as if he was about to face a firing squad. A small tear wrestled its way from his eye, and he buried his head in his hands. When he mustered up the courage to speak, he raised his head and looked into her eyes.

"I'd never worried about the lie before because not having had a father didn't seem to matter. But now, I'm scared I won't know how to be a father, so please promise me that you will help me." He gently set his head on her shoulder, exhaled immense relief, and stroked her belly. She laid her hand on his head and smiled with deep affection.

Gift

\ gift \

* something voluntarily transferred by one person to another without compensation
* the act, right, or power of giving

GIFT

It's always fun to receive a surprise from someone you get to unwrap, or...

HE WAS THE LOVE OF her mid-20s life. The four glorious years, for the most part, indicated a dream relationship. Her man was a kind, intense and hard working gent. However, feelings of doubt and uncertainty began to occupy her thoughts, and the bliss she'd felt began to ebb away. Love, even deeply connected love, often fades for any number of reasons and the human spirit can turn cold so fast. She'd seen this firsthand from unexpected outbursts between her parents.

On short notice she had to take a business trip, and without any warning, suddenly found herself attracted to another man, which freaked her out. As if lost in a dream, she found herself kissing this stranger, and the writing was 'on the wall'. Shortly after this encounter, she realized her feelings were not associated with him, but with desire for freedom, and she knew she couldn't hide this truth. On the plane ride home she pondered her boyfriend, a terrific man, who had done nothing to deserve this brief betrayal. A day after her return, she asked the love of her life for a two-week break. Confused, he respectfully agreed.

She refused to allow their relationship to become a charade like her parents, and after 14 days, she expressed that she did not have definitive answers and assured him he'd done nothing wrong. There was no yelling, no extra pain, no wasted time, but rather what most people refuse to do – just say, "goodbye."

Beauty

\ byü-tē \

* the quality or aggregate of qualities in a person or thing that gives pleasure to the senses or pleasurably exalts the mind or spirit; loveliness

BEAUTY

The sheer visual of vistas, sunsets, monuments and the Grand Canyon, or...

THE CONTRACTIONS WERE NOW MORE horrible than even he could have imagined. The room felt cold and stark, but he was right by her side, humming in her ear his faith and unconditional love. She perspired profusely, but continued to push while wracked with pain. For hours she struggled, her muscles twisted inside, appearing as if she were being beaten and kicked.

He tried desperately to comfort her, but looked away to hide his anguish when a searing yelp escaped her lips. It sounded like something was going to rip through her back. As the doctor pressed her for another calculated push, he continued to hum in her ear and dab her forehead with a cool cloth. Now it was more difficult for her to push, and it seemed as though her entire pelvis might collapse after enduring this process for six solid hours.

When the baby's head finally cleared the birth canal, she wailed in exultation, and tears trickled down their faces simultaneously. She lay silent, exuding the frailty of a limp dish rag as he tried not to think of the internal physical pain she must feel. The nurse entered and placed their son into her weak, but joyous, sweat-laden arms. She looked down at her child, the pain no longer present, with tears of joy. Her husband raised his camera, and regardless of the sweat, her disposition, the mess of her hair, and the disarray of the room, she still managed a smile.

Respect

\ ri-spekt \

* high or special regard

RESPECT

To admire someone or be viewed by others much the same, or perhaps...

THE CRISP SUN ROSE AND a burst of frosty air escaped from his throat. Bundled and hidden, he sat motionless, very quiet. A mere whisper could shift the fragile air amidst the freshly fallen snow that blanketed the land. He set his rifle at the ready and viewed the forest tapestry through the scope.

Right on cue, a 14-point buck arrived at the crossing. This buck was a true vision of strength and beauty – it personified a hunter's prize. When the hunter reset his rifle, his coat sleeve rustled ever so slightly, and the buck's head snapped toward what seemed to be an inaudible sound.

The hunter's scope of the crosshairs framed the heart of the buck perfectly. Just as his finger began to pull the trigger – the buck suddenly turned and stared directly into the scope as if he could see his enemy. The startled hunter lifted his eyes from the scope just as a doe and fawn stepped out from behind the massive buck. They grazed peacefully, oblivious to the danger only 100 yards away, but the buck did not alter his eerie stare down with the hunter's scope and position.

Just then, his phone placed in front of him vibrated with a text message from his daughter. The hunter looked at the buck's family, looked back at his phone, lowered his rifle, and extended a slight nod. The buck turned to go, glanced back one more time, and steered his family into the deep woods.

Wedding

\ we-diŋ \

* an act, process, or instance of joining in close association

WEDDING

A ceremony to end all ceremonies and the union of a lifetime, or in this case...

A 50S MAN SLOWLY DESCENDED the staircase in his home constantly stopping to catch his breath. A cell phone rang and his wife bolted past him on the stairs, leaving him to hold onto the banister for a minute until she could retrieve him.

Only minutes later, she burst into tears and he could see they were tears of joy. The three-year wait for a heart transplant was officially over. Within a few days, the transplant was successful, and after post-op he returned home with a new lease on life. Now seated in his favorite chair he began to glance through the stack of newspapers over the last twelve days since the phone call came in.

A story caught his eye about a popular junior college athlete who had been the tragic victim of a hit and run about 50 miles away. He saw the date and noticed the accident had occurred the night before his joyous phone call. Against all odds, logic and the advice of his wife, he began a persistent search, which indeed exposed that he was now the owner of that young man's heart.

When he contacted the donor's family, they were reticent but finally agreed to meet him. Ultimately, the couple was happy to meet the benefactor of their child's tragic fate. Upon leaving, they slipped him a note. Within an hour with his wife at his side, he knelt before a headstone. He cut his finger and pressed it into the porous stone to leave a thumbprint and uttered, "Til death do us part."

Bed

\ bed \

* a piece of furniture on or in which to lie and sleep

BED

We do spend a third of our lives sleeping, but there are a lot of options...

THE PICTURESQUE GLOW OF A Southern sky at dusk gently lit the wrinkled old man's face while he sat on a small porch. Oh, how Grandpa so enjoyed these peaceful moments. He reached over and picked up an ancient handmade pillow that had been sewn by his wife. He slid the cushion into place behind his head and slowly started to push the antiquated, rickety porch swing into steady motion.

Grandpa's hand slowly stroked the hair on top of his three year-old granddaughter's head, which rested safely and content in his lap, with her legs hung over his well-purposed and crusty arms. Earlier that morning, the family had rescued a tiny black puppy from certain death at a nearby shelter, and that little ball of fur now snoozed peacefully in the child's lap with all fears allayed.

The sun gave its last gasp of light before officially saying 'good night' and the lightning bugs took over. The veteran outdoor dog, and master of the house, ascended to the porch and stared at the swing scene. The voice in Grandpa's mind drifted off to sleep and he slumped down. His chin landed just above his granddaughter's head. The elderly dog rested his head on Grandpa's foot and closed his eyes. Crickets were heard in perfect harmony as the swing came to a stop. Grandma appeared on the other side of the screen door, to see grandpa, the swing, the granddaughter, the puppy and the master dog in an inner-connected harmonious slumber.

Exercise

\ ek-sər-sīz \

* the act of bringing into play
  or realizing in action

EXERCISE

Feel free to go get your Cross-Fit on,
but the mind does rule the roost...

A 70-SOMETHING WOMAN SHUFFLED PAST the TV room and entered the remedial library, which were really a few tables, chairs and a sofa surrounded by a smattering of books. In the corner sat the senior facility's new laptop computer, an obvious overdue addition. But the computer world didn't appeal to 99% of the residents so it had remained virtually untouched since its arrival.

She sat down and pulled out a wrinkled letter from her grandson entitled 'Grandma's guide to the Internet.' She pressed the power button and a subtle but glowing smirk came over her face as the screen came alive with "Welcome." At first, her old fingers struggled with the keyboard, moving her finger on the mouse pad, and maneuvering the cursor, but his instructional notes were good.

She clicked on the Internet icon he had drawn for her as a picture and the screen filled with the browser interface. She typed in the one word website address he'd told her to input in that space at the top and pressed the return button. Boom, a new image filled the screen. The reflection from the screen lit up her eyes and she cried herself into laughter, as a few curious onlookers passed by the door. The screen revealed her family's website. She sat mesmerized for hours as morning turned to night until finally the staff came to shoo her away. She closed her eyes in bed, invigorated by the thought of this new activity and feeling 10 years younger.

Love

\ ləv \

* strong affection for another arising out of kinship or personal ties, i.e maternal love for a child
* attraction based on sexual desire; affection and tenderness felt by lovers
* affection based on admiration, benevolence, or common interests, i.e. love for old schoolmates
* an assurance of love, i.e. "give her my love"
* warm attachment, enthusiasm, or devotion, i.e. love of the sea

LOVE

A strong bond of adoration and care for another sure, but where is the ceiling...

A NEWS HEADLINE ON A computer screen at the ICU admin desk of a local hospital read: "Senator leads defiant charge against gay marriage." On cue, the doctor who had just exited the patient room of his son greeted that Senator, flanked by formidable security: "Well, the good news is he's going to live, but it was very, very close." The Senator weakly exhaled, sat down with a thud to release emotional weight, and stared off in a daze with a million thoughts.

The Senator finally proceeded to the waiting room to share the good news with his family as everyone leapt up with joy to hug one another. The father leaned in and whispered something to his wife. She pulled away from him, held his shoulders and gave an approving return with her eyes albeit a mix of sorrow, joy and concern. He then offered, "This has to be done, right now."

The father, who was an ultra-conservative senator, exited the hospital lobby elevator right into a sea of reporters who barked harsh questions at him. The Senator raised his hands to quell the media stampede and stated, "As much as I'd like my work in the public sector to stand for change, I must first change myself. My beliefs and attitude have likely caused this tragedy. My son is gay and his attempt at suicide changes my priorities. My hard line against those like him needs a better perspective. Therefore, I will not be seeking re-election."

Intelligence

\ in-te-lə-jən(t)s \

* the ability to learn or understand or to deal with new or trying situations; to reason and the skilled use of reason
* an intelligent entity, i.e. an angel
* intelligent minds or mind, i.e. cosmic intelligence
* the act of understanding

INTELLIGENCE

There is a standard IQ test administered all of the time. So much for people...

A YOUNG WOMAN PICKED UP her terrier's leash for his daily trip to the dog park and the energetic little guy went nuts. They departed the house, and when the car door opened, the pooch jumped straight in without hesitation. The following day, the same routine happened as it had for some two years. Most of the time, the pooch would even beat her to the car door and sit waiting. The following week, however, instead going to the park, they were headed out for his annual vaccinations.

She grabbed the leash, and performed the exact routine, with an excited terrier in tow. The SUV door opened, but her pooch would not jump in. She was totally stumped by his hesitancy, so she said, "C'mon boy...c'mon boy." The pooch moved closer and closer to the door, but refused to leap into the car. She even went so far as to place a dang treat on the car seat, but still, he did nothing...just sat there.

Naturally, she tried to alter her voice with a more light playful tone and was more gentle and reassuring. She attempted again. "C'mon boy... c'mon boy." This time she tugged on his leash, but the crafty terrier would not budge. She bent down and reached for him, and immediately he cowered away from the car. Rather than feeling anger, she grinned in absolute amazement and mumbled out loud to her, "You can't possibly know it's vet day." She picked him up and he whimpered, but there was no explanation forthcoming, no answer...he just knew.

Insurance

\ in-shur-ən(t)s \

* the business of insuring persons or property
* coverage by contract whereby one party undertakes to indemnify or guarantee another against loss by a specified contingency or peril

INSURANCE

It is important to protect the things we own, and our health, but what about...

JUST BELOW THE GRAND WINDOW of an upstairs suburban home, the sound of sex drowned out the sound of a pair of small hands busily engaged in picking the back door lock. Once in, the small feet ascended the interior steps, edging closer and closer to the bedroom as the entangled lovemaking continued.

The bedside table was decorated with a few highbrow photos of prominent politicians. The naked bodies were thoroughly engaged in their ritual, while through the crack of the open door a phone camera recorded all. Names were called out in ecstasy and faces were exposed.

Moments later, a teenage boy exited the house. When he arrived back home, he found his mother sitting alone. He said, “Mommy.” She looked up, her face bruised with fresh tears, which she quickly wiped away. Near the sofa was a picture of her with the man from the bedroom tryst as he hugged her deeply.

A few hours later, at a political rally, the next potential governor of the state stood before an excited crowd. The chief of police began to deliver an introduction on the candidate’s behalf. Just then, the politician’s phone vibrated with a text message. He glanced at the screen and noticed a video attachment. He clicked play and saw his afternoon sex affair in living color. The text message read, “You touch her again and this goes viral.”

View

\ vyü \

* extent or range of vision; sight
* the act of seeing or examining; inspection; survey

VIEW

Eyesight brings so much joy and texture into our lives, but what is below...

A YOUNG MAN, DRESSED APPROPRIATELY for his surroundings, carefully surveyed the location options as the sun began to set – his favorite time of day. The venue was more alive than expected with so many varied angles to watch as the daily hustle and bustle unknowingly passed. About 100 feet away, he was drawn to a distinct area where the light glistened between the foliage. He slowly ambled down to the area and sat lightly perched atop an uncomfortable rock.

The sunset created backlighting on his audience in a perfectly surreal way. Despite having witnessed this form of silent chaotic beauty before, today seemed different. Plant life swayed in rhythmic motion while clusters of physical life surrounded him, and yet, remained scarcely aware of his existence. What a rare experience of buoyant mayhem mixed with magical tranquility. This was the most majestic rush hour of his lifetime.

A new glimmer caught the periphery of his eye and he gently drifted about 60 feet further below. Cloisters of life were present in a color and shape menagerie he could not have previously imagined. He remained calm and still, with his weight suspended beneath the surface of the ocean, utterly mesmerized by its elegance. At that moment, Jacques Cousteau extracted his camera and began to shoot a vision of oceanic sea life never before seen in history.

Island

\ ī-lənd \

* a tract of land surrounded by water and smaller than a continent
* something resembling an island especially in its isolated or surrounded position
* a raised area within a thoroughfare, parking lot, or driveway used especially to separate or direct traffic
* a superstructure on the deck of a ship, such as an aircraft carrier
* a kitchen counter that is approachable from all sides

ISLAND

Sometimes we'd like to escape to one or even maybe own one, but what if...

JACKSON'S HIGH SCHOOL GRADUATION PARTY made its way back to the plantation-style residence. Every photo on every wall was a military tribute to the two oldest Thompson boys clad in their uniforms. Tommy was in the Air Force and Aaron was a proud Marine. The patriarch, Jim, who'd spent 27 years in the Army and achieved the rank of Major General, spoke in honor of his youngest son.

Virtually every family or life event included his father and brothers in military dress since they were 18. Jackson was lost in thought when his mother's voice snapped him back to present, "Come on Jackson; it's time." Some 50 family members and friends patiently waited for the teen to enter the room. When Jackson appeared, they launched into the song *God Bless America* as the American Flag graduation cake was ablaze with candles. The young graduate's face fell sullen and weighted.

Jackson's entire world turned back to him and he expressed his thanks, but then said, "Mom, Dad, Tommy, and Aaron – I love you all very much, and I hope that you'll continue to love me...but I have decided to pursue my calling, and it isn't the military." The room gasped – his mother started to cry – the two brothers moved to debate him, but immediately stood down following a simple gesture by the patriarch. The Major General looked deeply into his son's eyes for a long spell, offered an approving nod, and extended his hand to cement the acceptance.

Communication

\ kə-myü-nə-kā-shən \

* an act or instance of transmitting

COMMUNICATION

Eloquence and clarity are the foundation of life, but no cell phone needed here...

A VIBRANT YOUNG MAN ENTERED his home and was greeted by the exuberance of his loving dog. He slowly strolled into the kitchen, pulled out a few treats, and handed them to his pal. The dog retreated to his in-house bed near the corner by the TV and feverishly devoured the treats. He watched his best friend enjoying the treats and forced a smile through his glaringly deep level of sadness.

He disappeared quietly from the living room and slumped onto his bed. The tiny picture on his end table of a smiling couple snuggled in winter coats full of love with the dog by their side revealed better times with his now ex-girlfriend. His face weakened, his mouth quivered, and the gentle process of acceptance and breaking down began. The relationship was over, she was gone, and now he was back to a household of two – but at least they had each other.

Lost in thought, he looked up to realize his trusted best friend had jumped up onto the bed even though he knew this was a 'no – no.' His four-legged pal looked at him closely and then crept slowly toward him. Once beside him, he lay down and pushed his nose up under his hand, a paw resting on top of his leg. The young man cried a bit harder than before. The dog looked at him with eyes that carried uncanny and deep understanding. The man lightly gave him a pet and a small whimper of knowing escaped from the dog's mouth.

Truth

\ trüth \

* archaic; fidelity; constancy
* sincerity in action, character, and utterance
* fact; the body of real things, events, and facts; actuality

TRUTH

Integrity in life always matters, so be careful as it may turn on you...

OUTSIDE A SMALL TOWN HIGH school, a jerk senior and some pals approached some freshman who gawked at the pages of a nudie magazine. The main bully snatched the magazine from the kid and smacked the freshman's head with the magazine he'd just stolen. He laughed and said, "What's wrong with you? You know what's mine...mine, and what's yours is mine too, idiot." They laughed.

The kid fell to the ground and grasped at his jaw while his young pals just stood there petrified. A few hours later the senior bully sat alone in some nearby woods and intently gazed at the nudie magazine. Out of the blue, two older boys who had graduated the previous year now stood before the senior bully.

The bully considered running away, but there was no escape. One college boy snatched the magazine and smacked the bully in the jaw with it. The other older boys laughed, and the bully cried out, "Leave me alone!" The magazine slammed into his face again and another boy kicked him in the ribs. The bully began to cry.

"Come on," another college boy exclaimed, "Show us how tough you are." They tied the bully to the tree, stripped off his shirt, and painted 'Bully' on his chest and 'Wimp' on his forehead. The other college kid said, "Better call for your Mommy, tough guy." They took some phone camera shots with the nudie magazine beside him and left him alone in the dark.

Strength

\ streŋ(k)th \

* quality or state of being strong; capacity for exertion or endurance
* power to resist force; solidity; toughness

STRENGTH

Body builders or military personnel are valid symbols, but try this on for size...

IT WAS 10:00 P.M. ON A Saturday at a sexy club. A late 20s hottie hung out with her friends by a fireplace. When the waitress came over to take a drink order, the hottie said, "Non-alcoholic beer, please." The waitress shrugged her disapproval and walked off as the hottie bit her lip and stared into the fire.

Her mind began to auto-play the memory of her boyfriend slipping through her hands from the roof and killing him. His death led to her addiction from which she was now sober. The waitress then returned and snapped her back to the present.

She sipped on her non-beer and tried to chat with her friends, but for some reason on this night, she couldn't shake the memory. His face flashed before her eyes, and she blurted out a muffled scream that drew the attention of other patrons.

She excused herself and headed straight to the bar. She ordered a wine and was about to go off the rails when a striking man smiling kindly engaged her. His subtle sense of humor reminded her of her ex and she found some calm. She turned more toward him as they talked. When the bartender set the glass of white wine on the bar, her internal pain screamed to be released with one sip.

She wanted to lose herself and reclaim the sorrow – but she stopped. One of her friends came up to the bar, so she turned to her and said, "Here, I got this for you," and then turned her attention back to the striking man at the bar.

Mother

\ mə-thər \

* source; origin
* maternal tenderness or affection

MOTHER

They give the gift of life and the patience of parenthood, but here's a wrinkle...

THE JUNIOR HIGH SCHOOL DAY ended, and while kids exploded out of the building, a 13-year old girl was alone in the bathroom. She sat still paralyzed and completely embarrassed. Her mobile phone dinged, revealing a text message from her mother, who just happened to be out of town on a rare business occasion. She picked up the phone, her hands trembling, and quickly replied to her mother.

Across town, her father was not quite finished with a real important meeting. He felt his mobile phone vibrate. He pulled his phone out of his pocket and read his wife's text message, which caused him to wilt, as if he'd received a body blow from a boxer. He instantly raced to his superior's office, profusely apologized and bolted from the building driving frantically through traffic. He flew into a parking lot, jumped from the car and bounded into the store. Once inside, he was mildly confused, but got some help, found what he needed, quickly paid for the items, and bolted from the parking lot.

Now, two hours later, his car tires screeched to a halt in front of the empty school lot. He breached the door, encountered the security guard, explained the situation, and they exchanged a wry nod. He found the girls' restroom – bingo – and called out. Quietly, his daughter came to the door, her head hung low as if she was in trouble. He hugged her tight, handed over the bag with a feminine hygiene product and a spare pair of panties. She sweetly smiled through her tears.

Teacher

\ tē-chər \

* one who teaches; especially one whose occupation is to instruct

TEACHER

Wisdom doesn't see age, and often times, rises above education or experience...

ON A CRISP FALL DAY, an attractive femme moved to exit her sophomore college classroom. The second year student passed by the front row and turned her head ever so slightly to avoid the professor's stare. She headed toward her car briskly, as if she were late for an appointment.

She reached to open her car door when the professor arrived in a huff and with a dashing smile. He said, "I thought we were getting together?"

She replied, "Well yeah, but I have some important errands and I figured with finals week, you could use the extra time."

Intently he replied, "What do you mean? Our time is more important to me than anything." She stared right through him, paused, and then said, "I can't be your answer anymore. We have to stop seeing each other. This affair won't solve your marriage problems, and I don't want to participate anymore. Your wife is innocent and she deserves a fair end directly from you."

She offered a short hug and drove away. He was dumbfounded and was about to call her, but instead he stopped, took a moment, and absorbed the depth of her truth. Just then, another student sided up to him and sweetly said, "Professor, if you have a moment I could sure use a little advice." He gave his young protégé a wry smile and said, "I'm so sorry – I think I'm a bit short on advice right now."

Precious

\ pre-shəs \

* of great value or high price
* highly esteemed or cherished

PRECIOUS

Rare gemstones or a pile of kittens on an Internet video, but then there's this...

IN A DIMLY SUNLIT SAD hospital room, an elderly woman was at rest awaiting death's call. The nurse leaned down closely to her ear, but in full voice informed the woman that her family was now here. As her daughter quietly combed the hair from her face, the granddaughter said, "Hi, grandma." Grandma turned and said to her daughter, "It's okay, nurse. I've taken my pills for today."

The mother winced and once again, the granddaughter told her grandma what they had done today, how fun the rollercoaster was yesterday, and how cool it was exploring the woods. Suddenly, grandma sat upright, grasped the little girl's hand and said, "Yes, Janet, yes, we'll run into the woods and play."

The mother leaned down to her daughter and told her that her grandma thought she was one of her little childhood friends from long ago, and she told her not to be scared or upset. In a blink, the little girl took her grandma's hand, and said, "Yes, Grandma, I'm Janet. Let's go to the zoo and play with the animals."

The grandma looked right at the little girl, then up at her daughter who was now weeping, and said, "I am so lucky to have such great friends like you and Janet." The little girl took her mother's hand and placed it in her grandma's hand and held them both. "That's right, Grandma, we're all friends now, and we will get to play together forever and ever whenever you want."

Peace

\ pēs \

* a state of tranquility or quiet
* freedom from disquieting or oppressive thoughts or emotions
* harmony in personal relations

PEACE

When the noise stops, the storm ends or two foes cease the battle, because...

A CHARMING YOUNG COUPLE STROLLED through a vast meadow feeling the warmth of the sun as it beamed down like a spotlight on a stage. They spoke of life, their family and their future. She smiled lightly, but her glow was even more telling. She yearned for him to take her into his arms and show her that he felt the same way as she did for him over the last year.

The moment was upon them, and the timing was perfect, but he looked away from her gaze and asked if she was hungry. The moment was broken, and she felt thrown by his question. He insisted that they get back for the group feast. She was disappointed, but they departed the scene, held hands, and discussed trivial things. Still, he felt distracted to her.

They arrived at the picnic area where dozens of friends and family had gathered. Good cheer was plentiful, and when the meal was nearly complete, the young man stood to request the full attention of the group for an announcement. Seated next to him, his young woman's eyes lit up with anticipation, as she just knew that he's waited for this moment to ask for her hand in marriage.

When he spoke, his voice weak. He acknowledged that his disclosure would be a shock and disappointment, but he could no longer live in a private hell.

He said, "Mom...Dad, I'm gay."

Religion

\ ri-li-jən \

* the belief in a god or in a group of gods
* an organized system of beliefs, ceremonies, and rules used to worship a god or a group of gods
* an interest, a belief, or an activity that is very important to a person or group; the state of a religious person; the service and worship of God or the supernatural; commitment or devotion to religious faith or observance
* a personal set or institutionalized system of religious attitudes, beliefs, and practices

RELIGION

Often the name of your God or your faith,
but there's another type of worship...

AN IMMACULATE, HARDENED CATHEDRAL OF well-maintained grass belied the brutality that faced its inhabitants. Cut, bruised and bleeding hands slammed into the turf failing to support their owners. The bullhorn that pierced the afternoon sky was drowned out by the guttural barks of grown young men. Early August yielded 90-degree Fahrenheit temps and a 90% humidity index, aka, pure hell.

Some 55 young men gasped for another drop of air before the next whistle blew. A few of the more weakened ones crumbled to their knees, leaned over, and vomited into a bucket marked 'Winning is expensive.' Some retrieved energy fluid from an adjacent table, but were immediately summoned to return to their crew. Upon their return, they were greeted with jeers and "wimp" comments. Welcome to the dog days of what are referred to as "two-a-day practices" that require drive, commitment, and insanity.

On a simple Friday, onlookers watched with wry smiles and approving head nods. Helmets clashed, players barked, and pads cracked and skewered into each other so hard that shockwaves shuddered deep into their teammates' tired bodies. Water, blood, spit, sweat, pain, and injury were to be expected. If you couldn't handle it, then you'd be sent home. This is more than a ritual, and more than a tradition. This is called Southeastern Conference college football.

Time

\ tīm \

* the measured or measurable period during which an action, process, or condition exists or continues; duration
* a non-spatial continuum that is measured in terms of events which succeed one another from past through present to future

TIME

Many of us desire more and some of us don't use what we have, and also...

A MOBILE PHONE ALARM WOKE a man in his mid-40s on a Monday morning. During this season, darkness remained outside, so he turned on the light, barely managing to crack open his eyes. He rolled out of bed and his feet hit the chilly floor. Once vertical, he picked up his pace and ambled into his morning routine – coffee brewing, a must-check of his emails, and on to the shower.

As he grabbed a towel, he thought about his day and the big night that lay ahead of him. After his divorce, he'd recommitted to his business, being a good father and to getting his life back together. Tonight, he was going on a date for the first time in over two years. He was trying to look forward to it but, in truth, not so much.

While he fiddled with putting a new blade into his razor, he began to recall the first date with his ex-wife. He stopped in the moment and laughed at how young they both had been, and he recalled the life he had imagined he'd have with her. The future and forever just didn't quite last for their lifetime as expected.

Oddly, he felt a small tickle in his heart regarding that first date, born of that very same optimism about his future and what may be on the horizon. He picked up the shaving cream and expelled a blob. When he reached up to apply the pile of foam, for the first time this morning, he saw his face in the mirror. Right there, before his own eyes and just above his lip...was his first grey hair.

Pressure

\ pre-shər \

* burden of physical or mental distress
* constraint of circumstance; weight of social or economic imposition

PRESSURE

It's the air in your tires, maybe being as good as your cool friends, or...

A YOUNG NEWLYWED STROLLED THROUGH a grocery store. Underneath her smile, a slow negative churning in her stomach was in full turbulence mode. She stared at her shopping list and embarked on the task at hand. A few hours later, she arrived home, opened her cookbooks, and just kinda froze for ten minutes.

She retrieved the scribbled note from her purse marked 'Barb and Dan.' Directly across from the kitchen, the recent family wedding photos, which included both sets of parents, glared at her as if mocking the effort. Just then, it hit her, and she knew she was in over her head. Light tears wet her rosy cheeks.

She summoned her strength and found the proper recipe page. She slapped on her apron and exuded a smile. Boom, bang, splash! Drawers were opened and utensils were lined up. She cracked open a can of tomato sauce, grabbed the big butcher knife nearby, accepted her fate, and dove in with full force. Seven hours later, the house was filled with an authentic Sicilian culinary aroma.

She glanced at her watch, checked the stove, set the table, wheeled about and opened two bottles of dinner wine. Now, on with the dress and quickly styles her hair. She heard the doorbell and the sound of laughter as her husband walked in with her in-laws all set for their first home-cooked meal by 'the wife' since their marriage. Her hands trembled. She exhaled and headed to the door to greet her in-laws.

Passion

\ pa-shən \

* the state or capacity of being acted on by external agents or forces
* emotion; intense, driving, or overmastering feeling or convictions; an outbreak of anger
* ardent affection; love

PASSION

Maybe you find it in your art, your relationship or career, but what about...

IN A VERY RURAL SINGLE parent home at 8:30 a.m. on Saturday morning, a 12-year-old boy rolled out of bed. In the kitchen, he found a note from his mother, "Sorry kiddo, can't play Dad this morning. work needs me – so sorry." The boy crumpled up the note and slumped down, not angry, just bummed. His mother often times had to work two jobs. However, his favorite game wasn't popular with his friends, so there really wasn't anyone to call who'd be going his way to hitch a ride to practice.

So he slammed down breakfast, gathered his gear, and began the arduous hour-long practice preparation process. He stood up, carefully maneuvered the few stairs to the garage floor, reached for his bicycle, balanced himself alongside the house, and managed to push off for the very hilly impending 5-mile ride.

The awkward helmet and gloves made balancing all the more difficult. Now in full sweat mode, a few kids barked "idiot or loser" as they drove past. He arrived and entered, slowly struggling with his attire and bike. Some teammates started to laugh at him, but his coach, with great appreciation, immediately shut them down and said, "Fellas, our goalie has arrived, so let's get to work." The boy untangled his hockey skates from the handlebars with a strained, but excited smile.

Perfect

\ pər-fikt \

* being entirely without fault or defect; flawless
* satisfying all requirements

PERFECT

Math and science officially have real competition because sometimes...

THE PHONE RANG AND A female voice said, "Hey, hungry for pizza?" The man replied, "Sure, but I won't finish until like 9:30 p.m." She responded, "No problem at all." Promptly at 9:25 p.m., a lady entered through the side door with the aforementioned pizza. About 9:45 p.m., he finished up and joined her in his office. They exchanged a few brief stories and grabbed a slice.

She finished her first slice and closed the lid. She smiled and said, "I'm still really hungry" and began to disrobe. The pizza box and a mess of files were instantly shoved off the desk. For the next 30 minutes, they engaged in terrific, passionate sex everywhere in the office. She then excused herself and stepped out to go to the ladies room while he stumbled to get dressed and assess the mayhem. He was speechless that this long held fantasy had come into reality.

He wanted to be a gentleman and not rush her off, but he still had a large load of paperwork deadlines to meet, and there were all those files on the floor. He started to panic.

She returned minutes later, fully clothed and said, "Sorry, no time to finish the pizza because I'm meeting my girlfriend for a drink. Thanks for feeding me. Now that was a meal, and I'll see ya' later." She gave him a smooch and a wink, and he stood there unable to conceal the grin on his face.

Friend

\ frend \

* one attached to another by affection or esteem; acquaintance
* one that is not hostile; one that is of the same nation, party, or group

FRIEND

We tend to remember good times or tough times, the memories and laughter, but...

TWO COLLEGE DUDES STROLLED TOWARDS their apartment as one complained about a mid-back itch he'd had all damn day while the other remarked about an itch he couldn't seem to scratch. They laughed. A few hours later, one hollered for the other to "come here a sec" and his roomy reluctantly rose from the sofa.

In the bedroom stood his manly roommate in his underwear. After five minutes of embarrassed explanation, the truth was revealed. Seems that a little tiny tick bug had buried itself into the skin near his upper and inner buttocks area. His roommate's face appeared as if he'd seen a ghost. "You can't possibly expect me to remove that from there – I mean, I luv ya, bro...but are you kidding?" They just stood there, totally silent, and then burst into laughter at his situation. So...

Tick victim dude then handed his roomy the small tweezers, and the newly ordained proctology roomy agreed. Tick dude turned his back, dropped his drawers and bent over. His roomy winced, shook his head, begged him 'not to fart, please' and tried to ignore the hair and scrotum. Tick dude, "be sure you get the head with it." The victim reached back and revealed the predator. Tweezers poised, one deep breath, laser precision, and one swift yank, "Ow – wwww-ch!" Success. They burned the tick, high-fived one another, did three quick shots of whiskey and agreed to never speak of this incident...for as long as they lived.

Fight

\ fīt \

* to contend in battle or physical combat; to strive to overcome a person by blows or weapons
* to engage in boxing
* to put forth a determined effort

FIGHT

Maybe a few guys at a bar wanna go at each other, but this is the real deal...

A VERY HEAVYSET WOMAN TURNED up the music volume for her afternoon workout, and the pace of her feet on the treadmill quickened. Strewn across the living room were chewing gum wrappers, magazine articles, and a nutrition guide. She guzzled some water, stepped off the mechanical beast, and began her stretch.

She moved toward the kitchen when her phone rang. Then she chatted with her best friend about their impending 20-year reunion in Cabo San Lucas. The call ended, and she realized she was holding a big spoon and a gallon of ice cream. As if she'd been in a dreamlike hypnotic state, she couldn't even remember having picked them up. She screamed loudly, hurled the spoon and then instantly became very calm. She hit her phone, connected her Bluetooth speakers and the soundtrack from the movie Rocky began to play. She looked in the mirror, then at her dress, and snarled.

She reached for the freezer side door, grabbed two boxes of frozen cinnamon rolls, one box of frozen cake and grabbed what was left of the ice cream. Without a moment's hesitation, she flung her back door open, raced to the street to meet the trash collector just in time and tossed them in her bin. She returned to her living room as the song reached its climax and danced joyously with her arms raised. She eyed the sticky note on her refrigerator that read, "c'mon girl, 50 lbs. or bust by July 4, we can do this."

Power

\ pau(-ə)r \

* ability to act or produce an effect
* capacity for being acted upon or undergoing an effect
* legal or official authority, capacity, or right
* possession of control, authority, or influence over others
* one having such power, i.e. a sovereign state, a controlling group, an establishment
* often used in the phrase *the powers that be*
* archaic; a force of armed men
* chiefly dialectal; a large number or quantity

POWER

We think of kings, politicians and CEOs but there's this funny thing...

A FRANTIC MONDAY MORNING WAS the wrong time for a warning light to go off on the dashboard of her two-door luxury car. Irritated and about to be late for a very important meeting, she pulled into the closest garage that offered auto repair. She killed the engine, a faint knocking sound was heard, and she raced into a repair bay. A fairly typical looking auto mechanic walked out to greet her.

She quickly explained her situation, and he promised an estimate for her within two hours. "Excellent," she said. She called for transportation, signed the estimate form, and was gone. After her meeting, she tried to reach the mechanic, but there was no answer. Typical. So she returned to the garage, and upon arrival, the mechanic said he'd assessed that her water pump had failed as well as needing a new thermostat. The total cost, about $800, and take about five hours to complete.

A strong smirk escaped her face and "five hours – $800." She informed the mechanic that her father was a former race car driver. Having driven only five miles when she pulled over, it was virtually impossible for it to be both of those issues together, and either repair alone would take a max of 2-3 hours. She informed him that she was an attorney and the power of Internet reviews was quite real, especially when auto mechanics try to take advantage of females. The mechanic started to debate with her, but ultimately just looked at his feet...speechless.

Extraordinary

\ ik-stror-də-ner-ē, ek-strə-or – \

* going beyond what is usual, regular, or customary, i.e. extraordinary powers
* exceptional to a very marked extent, i.e. extraordinary beauty
* nonrecurring, i.e. financial transaction
* employed for or sent on a special function or service, i.e. an ambassador

EXTRAORDINARY

Above and beyond the norm is its mantra,
but sometimes even the unexpected...

IN A SMALL TOWN AMERICAN shopping mall, a white man entered a business for after-school youth entertainment. The man was inquiring about a certain section of the facility across the way when a large black man entered the facility. The white man glanced back at him with a disparaging look and continued on. Moments later, the white man saw his eight-year old son playing with a young black boy. The father barked, "Billy", and his child quickly stiffened in fear.

The white father reached his petrified son and said, "didn't I tell you not to ever play with...them?" The white adult gave the black child that very same disparaging look he gave the black man up front. Just then the black man from the front arrived on the scene. The black father looked at the white man and extended his hand to introduce himself. The white man refused, "Sorry, you're not my type" and turned to go. The little white boy said, "But Daddy, you said people not like us were bad, but he was good at the game, and having fun...just like me."

The black father looked at the white father, smiled and said, "Just like me. Huh, out of the mouths of kids." Just then, the little white boy broke from his father's briefly distracted grip, and ran over to the black boy to give him a hug, "See you tomorrow." The black father looked at the white father with a wry smile and said, "What are ya gonna do? I guess they're each other's play date type."

Unique

\ yu-nēk \

* being the only one; sole
* being without a like or equal; unequaled
* distinctively characteristic; peculiar

UNIQUE

One of a kind, a rarity for sure, but there can even be the truly unexpected...

A JUNIOR ATTORNEY FRESH OUT of law school with about $150,000 worth of student loans landed a position at a prestigious law firm. His first assignment was to review a recently tried case as practice as the firm had a big case on the docket. Supposedly, he was given access to the files to the case, but found a random sticky note that read, '8/14/16 – 9/30/16' documents moved to storage. Hmmm, he thought to himself, that's odd.

The young lawyer wanted his first assignment to be perfect so he hopped into the elevator and went to the lowest floor of their massive building to seek out the assistance of the Records Dept. clerk. It took over an hour to find the files, which were buried in a box. The junior attorney was so proud of himself.

After a week of working 16-hour days between the office and home, he opened a memo from an unmarked file folder. Upon first read, he could not believe it, but when he re-read it, he realized that this was a 'smoking gun'. The reality of the memo was evidence that what his new law firm had done was beyond wrong.

He made a copy and for a week attempted to continue doing his job, but he simply could not sleep. The next day, he knocked on an antiquated door in a lesser part of town, and an older lady answered. She said, "May I help you?" He simply replied, "No, I'm here to help you." He stated the name of his firm and handed her the memo. "I'm sorry for your loss. Take this because what we did was wrong."

7 DEADLY SINS THE ACTOR OVERCOMES

TITLETOWN
PUBLISHING

amazon

7 Deadly Sins The Actor Overcomes provides a unique approach to the profession of acting. The profession of acting is a vastly different conversation than the artistic desire to perform. One could argue the business of performance art may be the most difficult relationship you ever have with yourself. The desire to perform on stage is innate. The credibility afforded the actor who performs regularly on stage is well earned. However, your belief system about the art, when challenged by the desire to make money acting on camera, can be an emotional and psychological conundrum.

7 Deadly Sins The Actor Overcomes provides a fundamental toolkit to increase the likelihood of success in your on-camera acting career, while protecting the delicate balancing act of offering your psyche and soul as a product for sale. This work will also guide you through many of the emotional and philosophical traps that snare actors almost every day.

The Actors' Network
https://actors-network.com

The Actors' Network was founded by veteran television actor, Kevin E. West, in his Studio City apartment on May 1, 1991. From almost its inception, the organization was revered and respected and, after the *BackStage West* editorial spread in June of 1998, it exploded in popularity and attained an unparalleled industry reputation. We encourage you to read more about *The Actors' Network* awards and history.

On July 1, 2013 the organization officially transitioned into an "Online Only" entity and while the physical studio is now gone the Mission, "Help Us, Help You, Help All of Us", as well as the Credo, "Learn from the mistakes of others…you don't have time to make them all yourself" are still very much alive and well. Kevin E. West instead of giving Topical discussions in the studio has now created an amazing Webinar Library with 100, 15-minute discussions online.

The sole goal and mission of *The Actors' Network* has always been, and remains, to be the utmost in expertise and advice on the business of show business while maintaining the highest level of integrity. In doing all of the above we have been and still remain the pinnacle of show business education.

https://actors-network.com/abg/

ActorBizGuru is the industry's first on-demand educational video library, providing you with the answers you need to prepare and develop a successful performance career. *ABG's* diverse roster of veteran Hollywood professionals will give you the insight you need from directors, casting, managers and agents to build a successful career in your city as well as putting you years ahead when you make your move to Hollywood.

The *ActorBizGuru* library features answers to more than 500 questions, totalling almost 15,000 minutes of Hollywood education!

ActorBizGuru has been 20+ years in the making, and we now are able to provide you with the most intelligent level of performer business education found anywhere in the world. So sit back, watch, and let our expert content save you years of frustration as well as thousands of potentially wasted dollars.